Olympic National Park

Animals & Attractions

Billy Grinslott & Kinsey Marie Books

ISBN - 9781965098202

The chipmunk is small and bushy tailed. They live in many places in America. Chipmunks are small members of the squirrel family. They have pouches inside of their cheeks so they can carry food. They are very friendly and will take food from your hand.

There are many squirrels in the wild. They live in nests or a hole in a tree. You may see a red or gray squirrel. The most popular in Olympic is the Douglas squirrel. Squirrels are very acrobatic and can climb trees. Their favorite food is acorns. They like to collect acorns and eat them later.

Flying Squirrels don't fly like birds. They don't have wings. They have skin that is attached to their legs. When they jump from a tree, they spread their legs out and glide through the air. Most glides are 30 feet from tree to tree. But they can glide up to 150 feet.

Pee-ewe what is that stinky critter with the big bushy tail. It smells bad. Skunks are normally curious and friendly unless you scare them. If you scare them, they will flip their bushy tale at you and spray you with a smelly potion and it stinks.

Porcupines have sharp quills on their backs to help protect them. A porcupine can have up to 30 thousand quills, they are sharp and will stick you if you touch them. To communicate they make grunts and high-pitched noises. A group of porcupines is called a family.

Opossums or possums have strong tails and can hang from trees. One trick that a possum has, is when it feels danger is it will play dead. It will lay there and not move. Possums have white to gray face hair. Possums like to eat wood ticks. They are also immune to snakebites.

Raccoons like to come out at night. Their eyes are made so they can see in the dark. They are called masked bandits because they have a dark mask around their eyes, and they like to raid and eat out of trash cans at night.

Muskrats can hold their breath swim underwater for as long as 20 minutes. Their webbed hind feet act as paddles and they use their tail as a rudder to steer themselves. They can swim at a speed of up to 3 miles per hour. They can even swim backwards. Muskrats will also give a warning slap with their tail, similar to a beaver. They build huts out of sticks and weeds to live in.

Beavers use their teeth to cut and knock down trees. They build dams with them to block water, so they have a place to live and swim. They also eat wood. Beavers can stay underwater for about 8 minutes. Beavers slap their tails on the water to indicate danger. Beavers are the largest rodents in North America.

Otters have the thickest fur of any animal. The otter is one of the few mammals that use tools. A group of otters resting together is called a raft.

Otters primarily rely on their sense of touch, whiskers, and forepaws, in murky waters to locate food. Otters have built in pouches of loose skin under their forearms to stash extra food when diving.

This is a Gopher. Some people call them ground squirrels. Gophers are little excavators. Gophers are known for building complex underground tunnel systems. They use their front legs and sharp claws to push dirt out of their tunnels and onto the grass above. Gophers spend most of their time underground and only come out occasionally to feed on plants aboveground.

Marmots can't see very far. They are most active during the day because of their poor eyesight. They like to come out of their dens in the morning and afternoon. Marmots have rough fur, small ears, and short tails. Their strong feet and claws are built for digging holes in the dirt. They are nicknamed the whistle pig, for the high pitched chirp they make to warn other group members of potential Danger.

The weasel is the world's tiniest carnivore. There are hundreds of thousands of them about. They change color through the year. Weasels shed their winter fur in the summer for lighter fur in the summer. There are several kinds of weasel, and they are hard to spot.

The American Mink lives across most of North America and is a cat sized. Mink are very skilled climbers and swimmers. They prefer to keep to themselves. They communicate using odors, visual signals, and other sounds. They purr when they're happy. Mink are agile swimmers, and they often dive to find food

American martens are small animals, living on trees. They belong to the same group as skunks and weasels. The body of marten is slim, and legs are short. excellent climbers, which has earned them the nickname tree-cat. Apart from being excellent climbers, martens are also agile swimmers.

Fishers are native to North America. They hiss and growl when upset. They are closely related to badgers, mink, and otters. Fisher young are known as kits. Fishers are one of the few animals that eat porcupines. Fishers are also called pekan, pequam, wejack, and woolang.

Bobcats are frequently misidentified as a lynx. Bobcats are part of the lynx family, but they are smaller than a lynx with different markings.

The Lynx is larger than its relative the bobcat and has lighter fur and more spots than a bobcat. The lynx is more than twice the size of a house cat. Lynx have natural snowshoes for feet. Lynx hunt at night. Their tufted ears help to enhance hearing.

The mountain lion is one of the biggest cats in North America. The largest mountain lion ever recorded weighed 276 pounds. Mountain lions don't roar like other big cats they communicate in different ways, such as chirping, growling, shrieking, and even purring. The mountain lion is also known as a cougar.

There are several types of foxes in North America. This is a red fox. Females are called vixens. Red foxes have supersonic hearing. When afraid, red foxes grin or look like they are smiling. Red foxes front paws have five toes, while their hind feet only have four.

The coyote is bigger than a fox. Eastern coyotes are part wolf. Coyotes are great for pest control. They like to eat mice and rats. They can adapt and live almost anywhere, even in the city. They have a yip type of call when they communicate with each other.

The timber wolf, also known as the gray wolf, is the largest wolf in North America. Wolves are legendary because of their spine-tingling howl, which they use to communicate. Their territory size is 25 to 150 square miles. They like to roam in packs of 2 to 25 wolves. You can see gray wolves in the Park's western and northern river valleys.

Mountain goats can jump 12 feet in one leap. They like to live in high altitude environments. A mountain goats fur coat has a double layer that sheds in the summer and provides warmth in the winter. They have hooves designed to grip onto rocks to keep from falling.

Black Tailed have a black tail. They are active at dusk and dawn. During the day they rest near water. They live in higher areas during the summer and move to lower elevations during the winter. Black-tailed deer are reddish-brown in summer and brownish gray during winter.

Weighing in at up to 700 pounds, the North American Elk is one of the biggest deer species on earth. They can run as fast as 40 miles per hour. They can outrun horses. They make a cool bugling sound when communicating with other elk. It's fun to listen to them.

Black bears are the smallest members of the bear family in North America. Black Bears love to eat sweet things like berries, fruits, and vegetables. They are good climbers and fast runners. They usually sleep for long periods of time and hibernate during the winter.

Kalaloch and Ruby Beach are located on the southwest coast of the Olympic Peninsula. They are accessible off Highway 101. There is a large parking lot for Ruby beach with a short trail down to the beach. Kalaloch is one of the most visited areas of Olympic National Park. Ruby Beach is one of the most scenic beaches on the West Coast. Go at low tide to view several huge rock formations that are stunning.

The Hoh Rain Forest on the west side of Olympic National Park. The Hoh Rain Forest gets its name from the Hoh River that carves its way through the landscape to the Pacific Coast. One of the largest rainforests in America, it offers a tranquil area surrounded by lush greenery, old-growth trees. The distance of the hike depends on which trail you take.

Hurricane Ridge is a mountainous area in Olympic National Park. Hurricane Ridge is located 17 miles south of Port Angeles on Hurricane Ridge Road, off Mount Angeles Road. The ridge is open to hiking, skiing, and snowboarding and is one of the most visited sites in the park. Hurricane ridge is a high point where you can view the tops of the other mountains. During the hike you can see many wildflowers and animals along the way. Discover this 3.4-mile out-and-back trail considered a moderately challenging route.

Lake Crescent is about 18 miles west of Port Angeles. The pristine waters of this glacially carved lake make it an ideal destination for those in search of natural beauty with surrounding mountainous views. Lake Crescent has several hiking trails, some climb the surrounding mountains, and others explore the lowland forests and creeks. There are plenty of picnic areas around the lake. Boat launches are located at the east and west ends of the lake.

Sol Duc Falls. From the parking lot, the walk through old-growth forest to the Sol Duc Falls overlook is less than one mile. Depending on the water volume, Sol Duc Falls cascades 48 feet into a narrow, rocky canyon. There are various viewpoints of the waterfall, both upstream and down, as well as a bridge that crosses the river.

Quinault Rain Forest. The Quinault Valley is a wilderness gateway to alpine meadows, crystal clear lakes and ice-carved mountain peaks. The valley has a scenic loop drive and short trails through the rain forest. There is a short 1.3-mile loop. Longer hiking trails through the Olympic Wilderness follow the North Fork Quinault River.

Rialto Beach is accessible by Mora Road, off La Push Road. Rocky beaches, giant driftwood logs, and views of offshore islands are features that define Rialto Beach. Rialto Beach is one of the most popular and one of the most accessible. A short path leads to the beach and ocean views. In summer, there is a wheelchair accessible ramp on the path. Rialto is a great place to look for wildlife, otters, seals, pelicans and bald eagles. You may see gray whales migrating in summer.

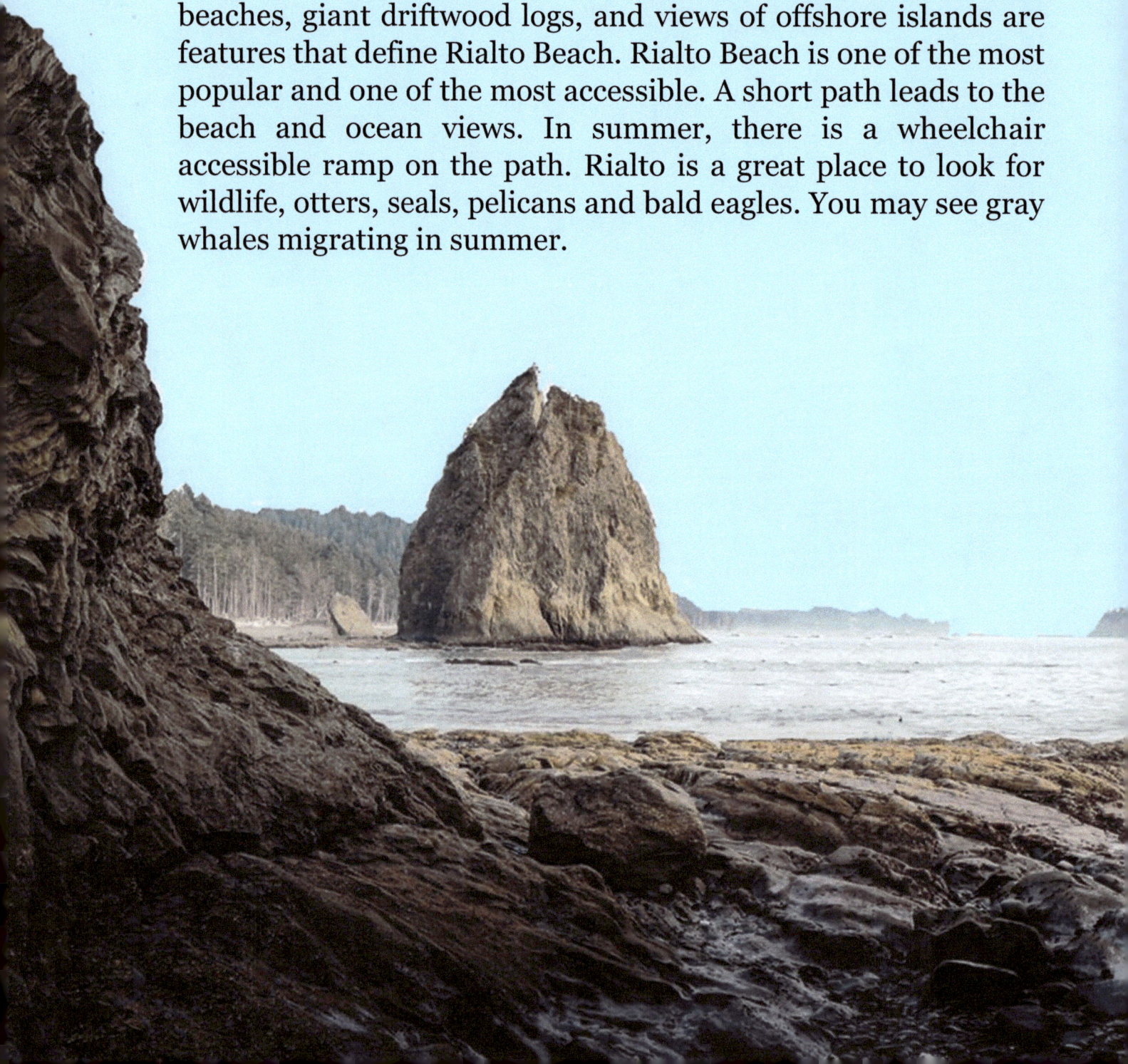

Second Beach Trail is a beautiful trail through a coastal forest that leads down to a Pacific beach. Second Beach is in La Push Washington. The trail to Second Beach starts at the Quileute Indian Reservation, and spans 1 mile before reaching the beach. Once you reach the beach, you will be rewarded with awesome ocean views and large rock formations. You can continue your sightseeing and walk by strolling along the beach.

The beautiful Olympic Peninsula loop drive extends more than 300 miles and offers a numerous amount of viewing opportunities, lakes, oceans, wildlife, rainforests, waterfalls and mountains. It offers many scenic stops and pull-offs along the way. The Olympic Peninsula Loop drive is a spectacular way to see the natural beauty and wildlife of Washington State.

Running beneath the Olympics mountains, the 200 miles of Hood Canal shoreline offers awesome scenic views. Several rivers and hundreds of lakes that are ideal for boating, kayaking, water skiing, fishing, or swimming. The Hood Canal area offers miles of hiking trails in the Olympic Mountain wilderness. With mountain streams, old growth forests to high ridge lines with breathtaking panoramic views of mountains.

Climbing Mount Olympus should only be attempted by experienced mountaineers, because it has snow and ice on it year-round. Mount Olympus is 7,980 feet tall. It is the tallest mountain in the Olympic Mountains. Depending on the weather, it can be seen from many spots. The Hoh River trail provides great views on clear days. The best view for those unable to hike close to it or climb it are from the Hurricane Ridge Road, south of Port Angeles.

Sol Duc Hot Springs are a great place to relax and take a swim. Sol Duc Hot Springs Resort offers three Mineral Hot Spring soaking pools and one Freshwater Pool. The warm springs are created by water that comes in contact with gasses from hot volcanic rocks. The heated water then rises to the surface along cracks and creates pools. Spend a night in a rustic, charming cabin and experience the Sol Duc relaxing hot springs.

Author Page

Billy Grinslott & Kinsey Marie Books

ISBN – 9781965098202

Thanks

www.ingramcontent.com/pod-product-compliance
Lightning Source LLC
Chambersburg PA
CBHW060852270326
41934CB00002B/102